THE SNACK SMASHER

AND OTHER REASONS WHY IT'S NOT MY FAULT

ATHENEUM BOOKS FOR YOUNG READERS
New York   London   Toronto   Sydney

Atheneum Books for Young Readers
An imprint of Simon & Schuster Children's Publishing Division
1230 Avenue of the Americas
New York, New York 10020

Book design by Michael McCartney
The text for this book is set in Goudy Old Style.
The illustrations for this book are rendered in pen and ink.
Manufactured in China
First Edition
10 9 8 7 6 5 4 3 2 1
Library of Congress Cataloging-in-Publication Data
Perry, Andrea.
The snack smasher and other reasons why it's not my fault / Andrea Perry.—1st ed.
p.   cm.
A collection of poems about the sneaky villains that cause life's little annoyances.
ISBN-13: 978-0-689-85469-9
ISBN-10: 0-689-85469-2
1. Children's poetry, American. I. Title.
PS3566.E69485S63 2007
811'.54—dc22   2006013924

For Dennis,
May you snore in my ears
for twenty more years
—A. P.

To Issy
—A. S.

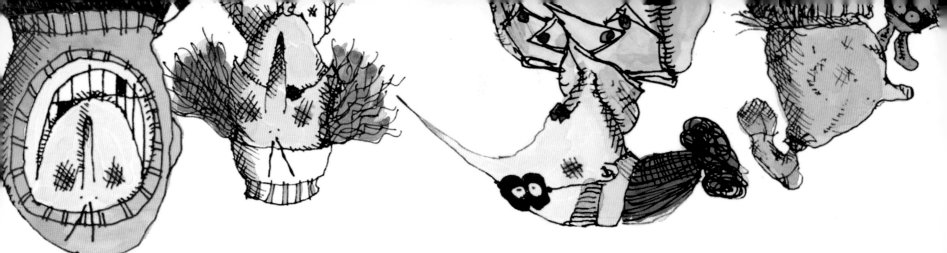

CONTENTS

Pleased
to Meet You?

Don't open these pages expecting to find
anyone generous, friendly, or kind,
for only the vilest of villains dwell here—
roughnecks whose ruthless intentions are clear;

scoundrels and scalawags given to crime;
dastardly deed doers all in their prime.
While some of them may seem familiar to you,
the others could fill up a hoodlum's Who's Who.
This book is jam-packed with the worst of the worst!
So who do you think you would like to meet first?

Snack Smasher

Pretzels,
peanuts,
popcorn—smashed.
Candy,
crackers,
cookies—bashed.
Malted,
mocha
munchies—crunched.

Salty,
spicy
snack food—punched.
Brussels sprouts,
liver, and
spinach—intact?
Dastardly
Snack Smasher
must have attacked!

Puzzle-Piece Eater

The Puzzle-Piece Eater
is one sneaky dude.
He'll ransack your closet
in search of fast food,
then steal puzzle pieces
to swallow unchewed.

(Though sometimes these creatures
will also include
a marble or checker
when they're in the mood.)
With this information
I have to conclude
that Puzzle-Piece Eaters
are creepy and rude.

The Scary-Hair Fairy

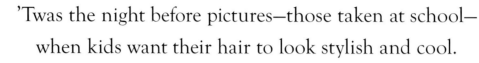

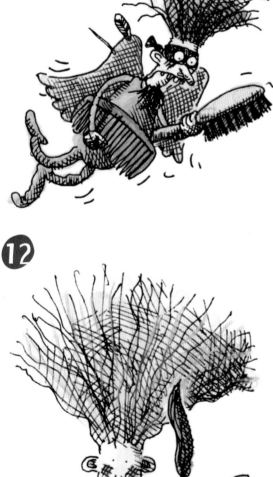

'Twas the night before pictures—those taken at school—
when kids want their hair to look stylish and cool.

The students were nestled in bed unaware
of what was about to become of their hair.

When up on the dresser top, who should appear,
but that messer of tresses photographers fear.

The Scary-Hair Fairy! That rascally knave!
That scoundrel whose magic makes hair misbehave.

More rapid than spritzing, he'll straighten your curls.
He'll give you six cowlicks and bangs all awhirl.

With a twist of his comb and mysterious gel,
you're helplessly under his hair-raising spell.

He'll tangle your ringlets. He'll snarl and he'll knot
and stiffen and crimp all your hair so it's taut.

And then he'll be off spreading split ends and frizz
to the next unsuspecting young Mister and Ms.

Yet as he's departing, his warning is clear.
He snickers with such a cold scalawag sneer.

"Tomorrow will bring you the bleak prospect of
a school picture only a mother could love!"

Horn Twister

Out in the pasture
all cows like to graze
unless the Horn Twister is near.
This meanie will mangle
the poor bovines' horns
and is therefore a figure to fear.

He creeps very close
to the heifer of choice,
then leaps from its tail to its back
and rotates both horns
one hundred degrees
so they're crooked and all out of whack.

When horns are turned backward
the cattle will OOM,
and their udders produce only KLIM.
Some cows have backed up
all the way to the barn
once they've been hornswoggled by him!

15

Cap-Napper
and
Lid Lifter

Cap-Napper! Lid Lifter! Duo of doom!
Don't let them in or they'll ravage your room!

Anyone leaving containers unscrewed
will get you-know-who in a lid-lifting mood.

They hide in your kitchen. They don't fool around.
They stash lids and caps where they'll never be found,

and then use their cunning precision and skill
to knock your jars over to splatter and spill.

Who else but these loons running loose in your house
would dump lemon yogurt all over your blouse?

Unstoppered bottles of syrup, shampoo,
and big tubes of toothpaste will ooze on your shoe.

If you're not more careful, this terrible twosome
will turn your clean home into something quite gruesome.

Don't leave lids alone! Always put your caps on!
And send a clear message: Cruel duo, be gone!

Wicked Waitress

She serves me spaghetti.

It twitches.

It wriggles.

Where could this have come from?

It slithers.

It jiggles.

What kind of a waitress
(demented?)
(irate?)
brings pasta to people,
alive
on a plate?

Ink Drinkers

Ink Drinkers are sly.
Ink Drinkers are daring.
They think that your pens
are theirs for the sharing.

They don't want to write
(their penmanship's awful).
They'd rather drink ink,
which should be unlawful.

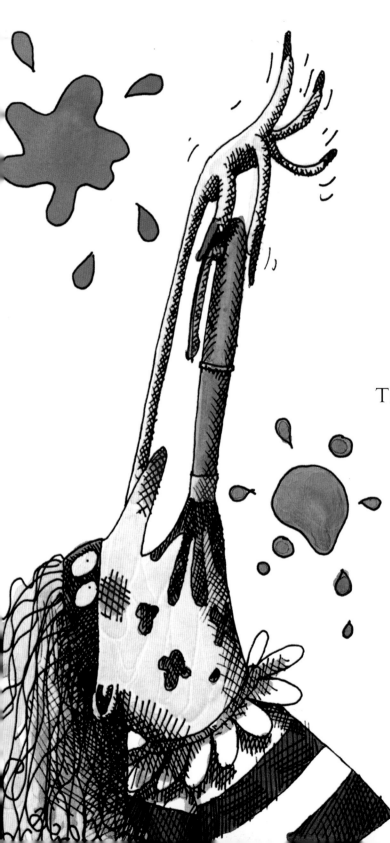

Brazenly perched on
a desktop or table,
they uncap and drain
as much as they're able.

Red, blue, or black ink?
There's none that they favor.
They'll guzzle and gulp
most any ink flavor.

The only sure way
to stop them, we think,
is to leave out a pen of
invisible ink.

The Snake Knotters

On your trip to the zoo, if the reptile display
has a sign reading CLOSED FOR UNTYING TODAY,
then certainly someone of snake-knotting fame
is most very likely the person to blame.

Nothing makes one of those Snake Knotters gladder
than tying a knot in an asp or an adder,
unless it's an extra-long python they've got,
that's twisted and bound in a big double knot.

They boast to their buddies that nobody knows
just how they can tie up those boas in bows,
and once it took zookeepers, spinning around,
an hour to get the sidewinders unwound!

You need not look further for villains much odder
than those who are known as the naughty Snake Knotters!

23

Snorist

That sound you can hear?

At night in the dark?

That isn't a sneeze, or a burp, or a bark?

It's loud and alarming?

It keeps you awake?

And causes your bed and your dresser to shake?

That sound is the Snorist.
It means that he chose
to sneak with his tuba inside your dad's nose.

He won't ever leave
or stop making noise
since being annoying is what he enjoys.

He's rude and uncouth,
a bothersome creep,
who wants to make sure no one gets any sleep.

He'll play on for hours—
six, seven, or more—
each song getting louder and worse than before.

There might be a lull,
but don't rest too soon . . .
the Snorist has merely switched to his bassoon!

Grumblebee

The Grumblebee stink bombs your posies
from lilies to pansies to rosies.

He's a vile, smelly bug,
a mean garden thug,
and a danger to bloom-sniffing nosies.

The Locker Destroyer

In every school building
there lurks an annoyer
more commonly known as
the Locker Destroyer.

She watches with rapture
as pupils deposit
their backpack belongings
in each metal closet.

Then once they've departed
and left her alone,
she wreaks the destruction
for which she is known.

Pencils, erasers,
and rulers go flying.
Papers are swirling
and fast multiplying.

Math books and lunch boxes,
mittens and hats,
jump, spin, and tumble
like crazed acrobats.

Graphs, maps, and note cards
are hurtled about.
Gym shorts and jackets
are turned inside out.

Not one single item
is left in its place,
not even an oboe
or clarinet case!

All students be cautious!
You may need protection
when lockers are opened
for teacher inspection!

Mistletoad

At holiday hooplas
make sure you're aware
of anything green overhead.

That sweet decoration
might very well be
the Mistletoad beastie instead.

As you're puckering up
for that one special kiss,
the Mistletoad swings down and flips.

It lands on your chin,
and before you can speak,
plants a sloppy wet smooch on your lips!

So watch who you're kissing;
you might start to shrink
and turn wartier than you once were.

This can be distressing
for party guests, but
it's what Mistletoads clearly prefer.

The Boot Remover

You lurk.
You look.
You see
the snow.

You plot.
You plan.
And then
you go.

You slink.
You sneak.
You creep.
You snatch.

You steal
our boots.
You're hard
to catch.

Why us?
Why boots?
Why now,
pray tell?

Bug off!
Be gone!
Get lost!
Farewell!

33